BUFFALO JOE
AND THE
UNDERWATER MATCHES

as recollected by
Grandpa Dan

Unlikely Publications Global
Orlando

All illustrations are believed to be from Buffalo Joe's own sketchbook. The drawings, covered in dust and worn by years of harsh weather, were discovered in an old barn. Their provenance cannot be proven definitively.

For more information, contact the publisher:
Unlikely Publications Global
www.unlikelypublicationsglobal.com

ISBN: 978-1-7374045-7-6
First edition: December 2022

DEDICATION

For my children and their children
and their children's children.

CONTENTS

Buffalo Joe...

Introduction

If you have a soul, then you have stories to tell. Some artists are highly skilled, but most of us create for fun and for the enjoyment of a small circle of family and friends. Either way, our stories make up who we are.

Oral storytelling is the highest form of the art. Stories handed down verbally from generation to generation have been proven to retain their accuracy. On the other hand, ancient manuscripts of the classics tend to be quite different from each other. Hearing a narrative allows us to slip into the action. We become full participants with the storyteller and the characters and feel we have a vital stake in the outcome.

I grew up in Nebraska. The midwestern plains are indelibly imprinted on my very being.

My children, on the other hand, grew up on the Indonesian side of the island of New Guinea. To say that growing up in the rainforest is different from their ancestral customs is the understatement of a lifetime. Each night, as my wife and I tucked my children in, they begged for another bedtime tale. They craved the knowledge of who I was as their father and where we fit in the world.

Now the kids are grown up and grandchildren grace our lives. The requests for stories waned in the intervening years but have now returned with a passion. My children want their children to connect with the collective family soul.

My grandchildren are at that sweet age where they willingly suspend their disbelief when faced with the ambiguities of life. Their inherent trust in the orator makes the narrative credible, even when their own experience doesn't confirm that the accounts could have happened as described. As happened with our children, when this current generation grows older, they'll understand and appreciate the joy of their skepticism. *Buffalo Joe* encourages us to live in, and relish, the tension between what we can grasp and what we can't quite figure out. We learn to trust our judgment while patiently waiting for resolution.

Today, we are well and truly an international family, living on several continents. No matter where we are and what we add to our identity through the rich experiences of cross-cultural living, our roots remain. Passing down the accounts of Buffalo Joe has resulted in all of our children embracing their Heartland heritage. All of them have a strong affinity for their home state even though most of them have only lived there for short stints.

Since Grandpa Dan can't physically tell bedtime stories to each grandchild, it seemed necessary to risk the virtues of oral tradition and reduce these recollections to writing. I hope putting them in print doesn't cause them to be lost. Memory guarantees longevity, but once a book is written, readers rely on the text to always be available and don't internalize the stories. May history not judge me too harshly for risking this for the love of my descendants.

For those of you outside the family, welcome to our small circle of friendship and intimacy! May you encounter these memories as a four-year-old. And to the best of your ability, tell the stories instead of reading them so that their genuineness can be preserved.

1

Buffalo Joe
and the Underwater Matches

Nebraska historians who have taken to musing about Buffalo Joe's extraordinary life agree that he was unknown to most people before he became famous. Other facts of his life may have faded from memory since Nebraska became a state, but that particular point has never been in dispute.

Some biographers speculate that Buffalo Joe was the very first person to arrive in Nebraska.

You, of course, know that's not possible. Neither the Nemaha, Ponca, Winnebago, Pawnee, Oto, Kiowa, Sac and Fox, or the other Native nations have legends of Buffalo Joe. This proves that he reached the state after their folklores were finalized. If he'd been in Nebraska from time immemorial, they surely would've mentioned him.

I seem to recall nothing of Buffalo Joe's birth or where it might have occurred. I wasn't there on the day of his arrival, so that makes perfect sense. You're probably thinking, "He must have been born somewhere!" and you're absolutely correct. That's another point upon which all credible historical researchers fully agree.

The first known story about Buffalo Joe comes from a time when he was unknown, but becoming known, and on his way to being well known. That's when people learned that he'd invented underwater matches. And it's a good thing he did, because those matches saved his life!

Buffalo Joe spent his early years walking to and fro throughout the Great Plains, seeing everything he laid his eyes on. He thought about everything he saw, so he was self-taught rather than formally educated. At the age of five, he was still quite illiterate, having never seen writing of any kind. In his sixth year, Buffalo Joe wandered south to Oklahoma and discovered the Heavener Runestone. It took him several minutes to decipher what those Viking runes meant because ancient Norse script is not as easy for illiterate children to interpret as you might assume. Plus, several inches of fine red silt had settled in the engravings over the centuries. After giving them a thorough dusting, Buffalo Joe was able to work out the prehistoric etchings. He sounded out the runes and translated them as, *We should have*

stayed up north. Buffalo Joe considered the Viking lore to be wise and made the decision at that tender age to live out his days in Nebraska.

Traveling back northward through Kansas in those very early days, Buffalo Joe noticed everything was lethargic. They were called "the early days" because the sunflowers had not yet awakened. They slept all day long, as if it were early in the day before sunrise! Their heads drooped and they couldn't seem to rouse themselves.

Buffalo Joe camped amid those prairie flowers for several weeks on his way back to Nebraska. He often talked aloud since there was no one else to chew the fat with. He discussed the newly found Scandinavian wisdom about Nebraska with himself, which took root in the sunflowers and planted a seed in their minds. They shook off their despondency when they realized there was better territory farther north.

To this day, every Kansas sunflower yearns to be one state farther north. Each summer morning, they raise their heads and look northward, straining to see over the curvature of the earth toward Nebraska. They start off looking toward the Missouri River and then slowly turn their faces westward  to gaze upon the entire state before sunset. When the sun goes down, they sullenly lower their heads until sunrise when they can enjoy Nebraska anew. Some people say Kansas sunflowers are tracking the sun, but you're a smart person and likely realize that ain't so. It's just that wherever the sun happens to be shining is the part of Nebraska with the best lighting.

Once he arrived back home, Buffalo Joe stayed in Nebraska as much as possible. He was twenty when he invented underwater matches. If you're wondering how the underwater matches were invented or what they are made of, the answer is I don't recollect any more than that he invented them and that they once saved his life. You can't make up parts of oral history that you don't know yerself!

Some say Buffalo Joe rediscovered the formula for Greek fire. But I assure you, he never went to Greece and all the fixins used in his matches were domestic. Of course, if you don't believe the story the way I tell it, you can arrange a visit to the Nebraska State Historical Society at the University of Nebraska campus in Lincoln and ask to see the underwater matches for yourself.

The first known use of the underwater matches was along about the year of the Great Salt Creek Flood. Buffalo Joe wasn't yet known as Buffalo Joe back then. His name before the flood was just Joe. When Salt Creek rose above its banks, he happened to be camping there, just outside of Lincoln. The floodwaters were cleverly pesky that year. They didn't jump right out of the creek bed in a way a body would notice. Had there been an abrupt flash flood, the future Lincolnites would've hopped to and sandbagged the banks to keep the stream in its place.

Instead, those sly waters snuck out of Salt Creek in nearly imperceptible slow motion. Joe was sleeping at the edge of the creek that night. A small trickle of water clambered noiselessly from the bank. Startled to see Joe's bare feet, the dribble nearly jumped back in the creek. Would that it had! That would've ended the flood and prevented the ravaging damage

of what was destined to become the state capital. No, that water, although surprised, kept it's cool. Nebraska is known, after all, for its abundance of cool water. The trickle pooled near Joe's feet and tickled his toes to see if he would wake up.

Joe was plumb tuckered out and, though he tossed a bit as his clothes dampened, he slept sounder than a Kansas sunflower. So, the trickle spread silently past him and flowed into town. After stealthily seeping under the front doors of homes, livery stables, hen houses, and bowling alleys, the creek cunningly rose without disturbing anyone's slumber.

When Joe finally sputtered awake, it was too late. He had just enough time to wrap himself in his buffalo-skin blanket and take a last gasp of air before he sank to the bottom of Salt Creek. He surely would've perished without his underwater matches, but when the waters subsided a few days later, Joe was still alive and kicking. He walked into Lincoln, shivering, wrapped in his buffalo skin. He passed the General Store owned by Lilac Lilly Kuwanawe's parents.

Lilac Lilly Kuwanawe was half Rhodesian and half Polynesian. One of her parents came from each country. They left their homes, one traveling north and the other headed south, and walked until they crossed the poles and eventually met in Nebraska. They both came from coffee-farming families, and each arrived in Lincoln with a small bag of roasted beans from their respective countries, which they used to open the General Store.

It wasn't coffee that Lilac Lilly Kuwanawe's parents smelled that morning, however. It was

Joe's bloated, sodden buffalo skin. Not only did the blanket smell, but the stench permeated Joe's pores and settled deep in his innards. Fortunately, Lilac Lilly (for that's what Buffalo Joe used as an affectionate moniker) was smelling-impaired and could not appreciate the aromas of either fresh coffee or acrid buffalo.

Joe and Lilac Lilly fell in love at first sight rather than love at first smell. Lilac Lilly's parents could see she wanted to court this fella something powerful. They invited him into the store to warm up over a cup of coffee. They were the ones to give him his nickname. Not because he was a buffalo hunter—which he wasn't. Not because he was someone who obviously knew the land and roved across it as a buffalo might—which he did. Not because he had curly brown hair like a buffalo—which he didn't. And not because he was strong and rugged like a buffalo—which he was. No, it was because he stank mightily. He reeked of buffalo. The name Buffalo Joe stuck to him for the rest of his life just as the smell did.

The fragrance turned out to be a blessing in disguise. After the coffee, Buffalo Joe parted from Lilac Lilly and her parents. He walked on down the street past the hen houses, wagon trains, and bowling alleys and came upon a flooded livery stable.

The owner of the livery stable was clearly frustrated. He'd been trying to sell a horse no one would buy. Buffalo Joe had been pondering the merits of purchasing a horse because, truth be told, he was tired from approximately nineteen years and three months of walking hither and yon across the land. Yes, he was twenty, but he didn't learn to walk until he was nine months old. A horse seemed like a good idea.

This particular horse was still damp from the deluge. Even if he had been dry, he still wouldn't have sold quickly, but the dampness heightened the challenge. Buffalo Joe bought him at a discount due to his one undesirable quality and rode him back to the General Store.

"Look!" he called out to Lilac Lilly and her parents, "This is my new horse, Old Paint."

Yes, you've figured it out. Old Paint wasn't named because he was dappled like old paint on a barn—which he wasn't. He wasn't named because his hooves were as crusty and hard as a tin bucket of black paint—which they were. And he wasn't named because he had a mane like a bristly horse-hair paintbrush—which he did. No, Old Paint smelled like a bucket of old paint! Especially when he was wet.

Buffalo Joe was not one to cast the first stone. Neither was Old Paint one to point fingers at unpleasant smells because, of course, he had no fingers. And Lilac Lilly was smelling-impaired, so the three of them were a match made in heaven.

Buffalo Joe's underwater matches, on the other hand, were not made in heaven, although one could easily contend that Nebraska is heaven on earth. That fact notwithstanding, Buffalo Joe fashioned the matches out of locally available earthly resources he encountered on his extensive travels through the Territory. And it's a lucky thing he did.

Over coffee that night, Buffalo Joe told Lilac Lilly the tale of how he survived the flood. After that last gasp of air, he sank to the bottom of Salt Creek. The buffalo skin kept him warm for an hour or two, but the water was much too cold at the bottom. The Creek had grown so deep that the surface was too far away for Buffalo Joe to swim to. Hypothermia was fixin' to set in as he tumbled head over heels with the current along the creek bed. As he banged into snags, Buffalo Joe grabbed pieces of driftwood until he had enough to make a campfire. He searched his pockets for the underwater matches. Although he'd been flung around like a rodeo cowboy with his hand caught in the rope after being thrown from the bull, the matches were still there!

Buffalo Joe struck the match, and it was truly waterproof enough to burn under water! The  driftwood campfire blazed away despite being driven, tossed, and bounced around by the torrent that entire day and into the next. Fortunately, Buffalo Joe could swim fast enough to keep pace with the fire as they jostled along the bottom of the swollen Salt Creek. Eventually, the water subsided enough that it was no longer too far a distance to swim to the surface.

I'd venture to say you're not inclined to believe this recollection is true. When I first heard the story, I didn't believe it was strictly factual either. But then I went to the Nebraska State Historical Society Museum and asked to see the matches. It's understandable for you to doubt until you go and see the underwater matches for yourself too.

2

BUFFALO JOE
AND THE PETRIFIED TORNADO

B uffalo Joe and Lilac Lilly were not extraordinarily different from other newlyweds in the Nebraska Territory or from newlyweds throughout the ages. They, like all who came before and since, commenced to setting up a home, working hard to put bread on the table, and giving each other goofy, starry-eyed looks. They were not *extraordinarily* different from other newlyweds, but they were *somewhat* different.

Most newlyweds set up their home by choosing decorations, curtains, and color schemes and strategically placing lace doilies on all the horizontal spaces in their house. Buffalo Joe and Lilac Lilly certainly admired a well-placed doily, but they had to literally set up their home by going out each morning to cut sod blocks to build it. They did pay close attention to

the color scheme of the earthen blocks. There were many natural tones to choose from, including browns, grays, reds, ochers, and the green marble streaks found in the upper layers of soil where the buffaloes had deposited their pies in more recent months. It is not common knowledge among city folk that North American bison were such discerning interior designers, willing to help neighborly people with their decorative conundrums.

After cutting each marble-streaked block, Buffalo Joe loaded it onto a large brick hod. To make the work easier, he hauled four hods at a time to the build site. He hefted one to each shoulder then squatted down and balanced two more on his lap, one on each thigh. He would then prance like a  Slavic dancer, kicking out his feet and propelling himself backward to the homestead with his load of sod blocks.

Buffalo Joe tried to go forward once, but the precarious nature of the blocks kept him unbalanced. The disproportionate weight caused him to tip to the right and run around and around in a tight circle for half that day trying to regain his balance. His spurs cut deeper and deeper into the earth with each revolution. By the time Buffalo Joe regained his equilibrium, he was thirty feet below the surface of the prairie and had struck water. You might think his day was wasted, but that's how Buffalo Joe invented running water.

Putting bread on the table wasn't any lighter of a task than setting up a house. Wheat was not common in Nebraska in those days. Instead, Lilac Lilly had to gather grain from the heads of wild prairie grasses and walk home carrying the harvest in her apron. From time to time, she would cross the plains at the same time that Buffalo Joe was dancing home with a load of sod blocks. On those occasions, as young women who are in love often do, she would join in the dance. Lilac Lilly would fling the grain from her apron high into the air to separate the chaff as it hung in the breeze. She watched the grains glint in the sunlight and swung her apron from side to side to catch the falling seeds. Buffalo Joe loved watching his new bride dance in a shower of sparkling confetti on his way home to his marble palace of buffalo poo.

Dancing to separate the chaff was not what made it hard to put bread on the table. Once Lilac Lilly got home, she had to pound the grain into flour. Each time she pounded the seeds, the flour got one pound heavier. It's easy math to calculate and I'm sure you're ciphering the figures in your head right now. If it took seventy-five pounds to pulverize the grain, the resulting flour weighed seventy-five pounds. It was a rare loaf of bread that came in at less than fifty pounds. No one would disagree that it's hard to put a fifty-pound loaf of bread on the table meal after meal.

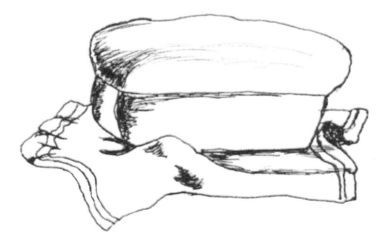

The young couple excelled at setting up their home and putting bread on the table, but they surpassed even the most outrageous expectations on the third chore of newlyweds: giving yer sweetie goofy, starry-eyed looks.

Old Paint often helped out with chores around the ranch. He couldn't do Slavic dance steps, but he would journey back and forth with Buffalo Joe all day. Old Paint enjoyed cantering beside his master as they set out each morning with fresh vigor. As the day wore on and the heat set in, he would lope back toward the homestead with his weary friend. With each passing day, Old Paint's hooves turned and tilled the soil until the track between the sod house and the open range became the best canter-lope patch in the county.

Buffalo Joe and Lilac Lilly won many a blue ribbon at the state fair in the following years in

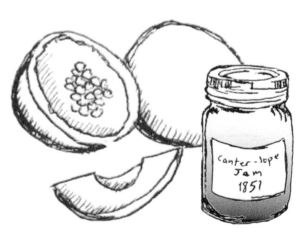

the melon category and a few lesser ribbons in the jams. They even took the old rinds from the canter-lopes and fashioned them into a carnival ride that children enjoy to this day. They called it a "Merry-Go-Rind."

You're probably thinking, "No, it's called the 'Merry-Go-Round!'" And you're not any more mistaken than the great majority of people in the world today. But history specifically asserts that on Old Paint's carousel, the rinds were fashioned into horse shapes in his honor and were not round at all.

One evening, Buffalo Joe and Old Paint were loping toward home. Lilac Lilly stood in the front yard holding that day's bread, which she was about to put on the table. Just as they reached her, Old Paint stumbled on a melon and careened into Buffalo Joe. The hod on Buffalo Joe's right thigh toppled off as he was about to kick and threw off the rhythm of the dance. Instead of kicking the air, he kicked the loaf of bread out of Lilac Lilly's hand. That day, it had taken her over 200 pounds to work the grain into a fine flour.

Buffalo Joe's toes and the bread's heel met with so much force that they both had to loaf around the house for several days before their wounds crusted over properly. In the moment of impact, Buffalo Joe's face wrinkled in pain and he saw stars. As I told you earlier, Buffalo Joe was not *extraordinarily* different from other newlyweds in how he gave his new bride goofy, starry-eyed looks, but he was *somewhat* different.

Eventually, Buffalo Joe and Lilac Lilly finished their sod house, stocked the larder with melons and jams, and made a bread box out of

two-by-fours and sixteen-penny nails to store their confectionaries. Theirs was the very first homestead in the entire country. I know you beg to differ, as any erudite Nebraskan knows that the first homestead in the nation is commemorated not in western Nebraska, but near Beatrice.

It is absolutely true that Homestead National Monument is technically the first homestead. The Homestead Act of 1862 allowed a person to claim 160 acres of land if they could reside on it continually for five years. Buffalo Joe was the very first homesteader to establish a ranch not too far from Beatrice, but unfortunately his claim didn't stay there.

Buffalo Joe and Lilac Lilly had already been living on their ranch a fair while prior to other homesteaders staking a claim. They were nearly ready to claim the title of first homestead along with the title for their land. On their way to the notary public's office to get the deed for their property officially stamped one fateful spring morning, the weather turned foul. A funnel cloud formed in the green sky. The twister touched down in the pasture near the canter-lope patch. Never had Buffalo Joe or Lilac Lilly seen such a tornado. They watched it suck up everything in its path. It pulled up the house, the larder, the garden, the pasture, the livestock, the well, and the water in the well all in one mighty heft.

Buffalo Joe sensed his one and only opportunity to save his ranch and acted without thought to his own safety. He left Lilac Lilly in the wagon, unhooked Old Paint, and chased after that tornado. They followed it from Beatrice all the way to western Nebraska over the ensuing days.

Most of the time, the twister was putting more distance between itself and its pursuers. Old Paint was a slow horse and could not hope to outpace the storm. Yet, as the cyclone pulled up gigantic rocks and boulders and ground them to dust, it began to lose speed. The more the funnel cloud packed up with the tons of topsoil it tore from the terrain, the more it weaved and staggered across the plains. By the time Buffalo

Joe and Old Paint reached Thedford, they were gaining on the storm. The tornado churned unhurriedly, then leisurely, then sluggishly, until it came to a complete standstill in the Panhandle. The storm had petrified into a funnel of solid rock and soil.

Buffalo Joe and Old Paint caught up with the tornado while it was still warm from the friction of all the smashing boulders. It had kept its funnel shape as it petrified and stood perfectly balanced upon a single grain of sand. The storm cloud spread out over a mile wide at the top.

Buffalo Joe and Old Paint deliberated how they might climb the inverted walls of the newly formed butte to see if their ranch had survived the journey. Eventually Buffalo Joe decided to unshod Old Paint's hooves and replace his shoes with halves of a  prickly-pear cactus. While the horseshoes required nails to keep them on, the sap from the prickly pears functioned as glue to keep the cactus pads in place. The nasty needles acted like cleats, so Old Paint was able to find purchase in the hardening, but still pliable, walls of the butte. Buffalo Joe tied himself to the saddle and rode somewhat upside down straight up the rock wall.

Half-way up, dust mixed into the cactus sap and the prickly-pear pads began to peel off. Old Paint scrabbled as best he could, but he finally fell back down to the ground. His hindquarters landed atop the cactus that had supplied his temporary shoes. The ensuing sensation made Old Paint jump so high that he cleared the top edge of the petrified tornado and landed in the middle of the plateau. To this day, Old Paint holds the record for the highest equestrian jump, but the purposeful use of cactus in horse jumping has since been banned along with other performance-enhancing substances.

When Buffalo Joe and Old Paint landed on top of the petrified tornado, they realize their good fortune. Because the ranch had been picked up first, it had floated to the top of the twister and remained there as the lower regions filled in below. When the tornado petrified, the ranch came to rest on the newly formed mesa atop the butte. True, the homestead was catawampus and no longer square with the meridians of longitude and latitude, but it had settled on its perch with nary a smidgen of damage.

As you travel through the West, you'll see various and sundry buttes formed from primeval cataclysms. The youngest circular butte in Nebraska is the petrified tornado. It stands out from all the rest. As it eroded over the years, it lost some of its pure funnel shape and widened significantly at the base. Yet, there's still at least one inverted wall where you can see the holes from Old Paint's cactus-spine shoes on the lower half.

If that tornado had waited an hour longer to strike, Buffalo Joe would've had the honor of being the first homesteader. But since the deed wasn't stamped, sealed, and notarized prior to lift off, the five years started over again in the new location and a homesteader in Beatrice claimed that accolade. If you visit Homestead National

Monument and contend that Buffalo Joe and the Petrified Tornado is the real first homestead story, they'll act as if you're spinning a yarn. They might not know history properly, but more'n likely they want to suppress the knowledge to keep the acclaim for themselves.

You may be tempted to believe what the folks in Beatrice say, or you may think this story is untrue even without their confounding of the facts. I didn't believe the tale either until I saw the underwater matches. You might not want to take full stock in it until you've seen them too.

3

Buffalo Joe
and the Upside-Down Rainclouds

Some people say silly things about Nebraska, like, "If you don't like the weather, wait five minutes and it'll change." Buffalo Joe knew that warn't necessarily true. Although it was factual that a storm could come up quickly, weather patterns were often stubborn, like senile old folks stuck in their ways. "Change?" the humidity might grumble, "Who needs change? Why, we've always done it this way. If it ain't broke, don't fix it." The weather in the Nebraska Panhandle was acting real senile one particular year. Buffalo Joe disapproved of its constant sunny disposition that summer and determined that it needed some firm persuasion.

Water is the stuff of life. It's essential for splashing, swimming, playing Marco Polo, and making water balloons and snow globes. It's needed to slake a cowboy's thirst, too. The weather was so stubbornly dry that year that Buffalo Joe and everyone else was running out of water. All of Nebraska was in a bad way. Crops failed, cattle panted like dogs, and mice were chewing through all the snow globes and guzzling them dry. It was so hot and dry it felt as if the Panhandle was frying on a stovetop.

As you are aware, I'm sure, it's not often that a river starts and ends in the same state. Normally it flows across two or three or even a dozen state lines. This is true no matter if the water comes from an underground spring or falls from above in the form of rain, snow, sleet, hail, or water balloons. Either way, when water reaches the surface of the ground, 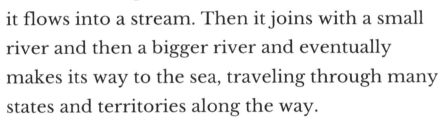 it flows into a stream. Then it joins with a small river and then a bigger river and eventually makes its way to the sea, traveling through many states and territories along the way.

Nebraska gets its water from rainclouds that form out west, way back behind the Rocky Mountains. The breezes blow the clouds up the western slopes of Colorado and Wyoming. Nowadays, when a cloud reaches the tip-top of the mountain peaks, the whole thing tips over and comes racing down the eastern slopes of the Rockies toward the Nebraska line. The rain that falls on the eastern side of the mountains ends up in the Missouri River, having flowed down the Niobrara River, the Nishnabotna, the Loop, the Big Blue, the South Fork of the Republican, Lost Creek, Calumet Creek, Cottonwood Creek or any one of the other beautiful waterways of the Territory.

From the mighty Missouri River, the rain drains into the Gulf of Mexico and ocean currents take it to the farthest tip of Argentina,

known as Tierra del Fuego. As all cowboys and Argentine gauchos know, Tierra del Fuego means "Land of Fire." As the water laps in waves against the shore of the Land of Fire, it heats up and boils. Buffalo Joe often remarked that the water went "Out of the Frying Panhandle and into the Fire." The steam from the boiling water wafts into the sky and floats back toward North

America, where it once again forms rainclouds on the western slopes of the Rockies.

The problem for Buffalo Joe that dry year wasn't that there weren't rainclouds. The problem was that all the rainclouds teetered on the tip-top of the Rocky Mountains and then flipped over and slid down the ridge on their backsides, just like a young'un does after climbing a ladder up a slide in the school yard. Young'uns don't usually slide down on their bellies. No sir! They slide feet first on their hindsides. And that's what the clouds were doing. They landed on the Nebraska Plains upside down.

There was plenty of rain in them clouds, but they rained on the wrong side—straight up in the air! All that refreshing rain fell up to the heavens instead of down on the crops and the rivers. The moon and stars got soaked and grew like weeds, but the prairie withered.

Buffalo Joe didn't need more stars—there were already more than he could count. He needed water so the cattle could stop panting and the mice would stop drinking Lilac Lilly's snow

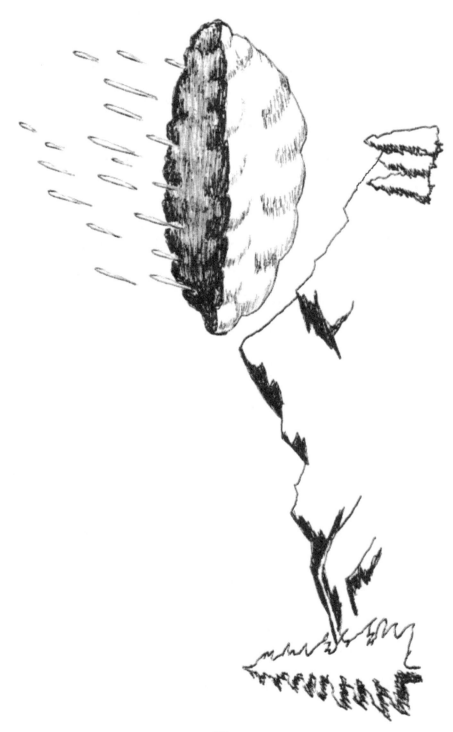

globes dry. Something was definitely broke with those upside-down clouds and needed to be fixed. Buffalo Joe decided that it was up to him and Old Paint to be the agents of change.

The next morning at sunrise, Buffalo Joe saddled up Old Paint, adjusted his stirrups, looped his lasso over the saddle horn, filled his canteen with the water from the last snow globe, and headed west toward the mountains. When he reached the feet of the Rockies, Buffalo Joe lassoed the first raincloud that poked its nose over the ranges, just like he roped calves at

branding time. He tied the end of his rope onto the saddle horn and Old Paint pulled with all his might, forcing the nose of that thunderhead down toward the Nebraska plains. They worked at it steadily for months. Not a single cloud was allowed to flip upside down as long as Buffalo Joe and Old Paint wrangled them.

It took quite some time for all the clouds to go through the hydrological cycle and encounter Buffalo Joe's lasso. After being roped a few times each, the clouds got to learnin' to come over right side up on their own. Once rainclouds started arriving in Nebraska right-side-up, the drought ended. Rain watered the parched prairie and, although there are still occasional droughts, no new stars have cropped up in the sky since Buffalo Joe and Old Paint's heroic efforts.

Now, you may think I've made this story up. I sure did suspect it was fictional when I first heard it. But then I saw the underwater matches. When you see the underwater matches, you'll believe it too.

4

BUFFALO JOE
AND THE PORCUPINE CONES

There weren't many trees in Nebraska in Buffalo Joe's day, but one afternoon a tall, magnificent pine caught his attention. At first glance, it appeared to be just like any other pine in the Territory. But there was an important difference about this particular tree. All the other conifers that Buffalo Joe had encountered up to that moment grew pinecones. This tree sprouted porcupine cones!

There's some general confusion about the difference between pine, spruce, and fir trees. Buffalo Joe was not confounded by those subtleties. The firs in western Nebraska had soft, smooth bark, and when you stroked their fir-y trunks as the wind blew through the needles, the trees purred in appreciation.

The spruce were known to be useful trees. When Lilac Lilly tapped the sap from their trunks and used it to scrub the laundry, the clothes came out looking particularly snappy. On special occasions like going to church or attending a square dance, Buffalo Joe and Lilac Lilly would don those dapper sap-laundered duds. People began to ask about their clothes-washing habits so that they, too, could get all spruced up.

Since Nebraska pines normally had pinecones, when Buffalo Joe saw the tall tree covered in balls of quills, he reigned Old Paint over for a closer look. At the tip of most every branch grew a porcupine cone rolled into a ball. As Buffalo Joe reached out to pluck one, the  sharp quills perforated even the hard-won callouses of his fingers. In an instant, the porcupine cone snapped itself off the tree and dropped to the ground. It didn't stick around long enough to play dead. No sir! It stuck out its little legs and scurried off. Buffalo Joe was even quicker, and he lassoed the little porcupine cone before it scampered into the brush and carefully tucked it into Old Paint's saddlebags.

The porcupine cone was a curious little creature. It wasn't long before he started feeling comfortable nestled in that deep, dark saddlebag, and he got mighty curious. First, he stuck his nose out. Then his whole body crept out. When Buffalo Joe turned around to check on him, the porcupine cone tried to burrow under Old Paint's saddle blanket. Talk about a bur under the saddle! Those quills were longer and sharper than any cocklebur you've ever tangled with. Old Paint hadn't experienced so much pain since he scaled the Petrified Tornado. He never fully trusted porcupine cones from that day forward. Buffalo Joe, however, found that they were like fir trees. If you stroked them as the wind blew through their quills, they purred with affection.

Within a few weeks, Buffalo Joe rounded up a small herd of porcupine cones and kept them in a pen at the ranch. Porcupine cones are part animal and part plant. They play and forage like normal rodents until late autumn. Then they dig burrows to hibernate in during the winter, which is when the plant phase of their lifecycle kicks in. Rather than emerging with other mammals in the spring, porcupine cones sprout into saplings.

Lumber was scarce in those days, so farmers needed to plant trees. Buffalo Joe trained the porcupine cones to dig their burrows in rows, and within a couple years he had a stand of pine trees that made a mighty fine wind break. The mature trees could be milled into lumber should he and Lilac Lilly ever desire to upgrade from their sod home.

Pine needles made the best sewing needles of any conifer. Lilac Lilly found porcupine cone quills better still for darning socks and patching petticoats. The porcupine cones eventually grew so tame they'd let her pluck a fresh quill each time a garment needed mending. Some of the cleverer ones would even thread the needle for her.

Buffalo Joe went out to feed the porcupine cones in their pen each day at sunrise and sunset.

They didn't need much fodder because they foraged with the chickens. Buffalo Joe's chickens were as unusual as the porcupine cones. They, too, had a plant-animal lifecycle. Instead of laying eggs, they produced chickpeas. Lilac Lilly gathered the chickpeas each morning as vegetables for her home-cooked vittles.

It wasn't long before the porcupine cones and chickpea chickens scratched and scraped away the top layer of soil in their pen. One evening, when Buffalo Joe came to supplement their daily dietary intake with some silage, he noticed the tips of bones sticking out of the earth. He was every bit as curious as the porcupine cone that became the burr under Old Paint's saddle.

With considerable effort, he soon unearthed a massive skull and a pair of tusks.

Today, everyone knows that Morrill Hall, on the campus of the University of Nebraska, is home to the largest woolly mammoth on display anywhere in the world. But Buffalo Joe excavated the first pachyderm in the Territory.

As luck would have it, Buffalo Joe and Lilac Lilly had a job just then writing a weekly newspaper advice column for star-crossed lovers. They explained all the intricacies and subtleties of gazing at your sweetie with starry eyes and a goofy smile, which doesn't come naturally to everyone. The week he uncovered the wooly mammoth, Buffalo Joe plucked a fresh quill and scribed a letter to their newspaper editor in

 eastern Nebraska describing the fossil find instead. Although skeletons of that magnitude uncovered by chickens scratching for bugs were later documented throughout the state, his editor took it to be a hoax. He expressed his mammoth-sized disappointment by truncating Buffalo Joe and Lilac Lilly's advice column contract while muttering "Tusk, tusk, tusk" under his breath.

Much to his eternal consternation, Buffalo Joe's firing from the newspaper led to many young people suffering from unrequited love. Young men lost hope in their amorous affections and moved to Minnesota to become the famed bachelor farmers so prevalent in that state. A love-sick paleontologist suffered the most from losing Buffalo Joe's sage advice. He wanted to be both engaged in a dig and engaged to be married. He chose to make his fortune first, before asking his beloved to become his betrothed, thinking his earnings would provide extra incentive for her to say yes. Without Buffalo Joe and Lilac Lilly's guidance, he lost the girl he fancied to a rival suitor who flattered her with longer, starrier gazes. The heartbroken paleontologist became so blue that his tears muddied the fossil pit, and he could no longer dig. He decided to run off and join the circus instead, where he was engaged as an elephant trainer in training.

If you are ever forced to choose between paleontology and love, as so many young people are, you might consider the example of the porcupine cone. In the warm months, it's as hard to tell a normal porcupine from a porcupine cone as it is to differentiate between true love and youthful infatuation. The only way to tell one from the other for certain is to let it hibernate and then wait until spring to see whether it wakes up and runs away or sprouts.

Buffalo Joe never could figure if woolly mammoths had a plant cycle or not. To this day we don't know for sure because they're extinct. Some say that, by a strict definition, mammoths are now all vegetative and we should actually be wondering whether they had an animal phase. The next time you come across a porcupine cone, stroke it gently to see if it purrs in appreciation. But be very careful, or you could end up in as much pain as Old Paint!

You may not believe this story. Honestly, I didn't think it was true when I originally heard it either. But then I saw the underwater matches. When you see the underwater matches for yourself, you'll know if it's true.

5

BUFFALO JOE
AND THE MOON DIAMONDS

A unique gem can be found infrequently in the rockier parts of the Nebraska Badlands, especially around what has become known as Toadstool Park. It is the rarest, most precious of all currently known gemstones—more costly than twenty-karat diamonds set in Black Hills gold and rarer than a Democrat winning a presidential general election in western Nebraska. Moon diamonds were scarce indeed!

Buffalo Joe and Lilac Lilly Kuwanawe were fixin' to celebrate their seventeenth wedding anniversary. Or was it their eighteenth? Nineteenth? No one knew for sure, least of all the happy couple. Time passed so slowly back then, one year merged into another without anyone taking much notice, and timekeeping was extra complicated in Nebraska in Buffalo Joe's day. Most places in the world are familiar with leap years, where the calendar sprouts an extra day to sync up with the sun. But out west they had to occasionally have skip years, jumping forward a whole year to recalibrate things. The years 1857, 1872, and half of 1891 (February 4th to August 23rd)

got skipped right over to catch up with the rest of the country.

To this day, you'll not see any pennies, nickels, dimes, quarters, or 37¢ pieces from those years in circulation because the US Mint didn't produce coins for the Territory in the skip years. You can test this out by making change for a dollar anywhere in the state. I promise you'll never receive a coin from the two-and-a-half skip years, which irrefutably proves those years never existed in western Nebraska. You might see those coins circulating in other parts of the nation because the Mint did strike coins for states that didn't observe skip years, but you won't find them anywhere between Ord and Scottsbluff!

It didn't really matter which anniversary Buffalo Joe and Lilac Lilly were celebrating anyway. Buffalo Joe always showed his appreciation and affection for his wife with a special gift. That year he intended to make her a diamond necklace. And not just any kind of diamond necklace either—he was going to mine for moon diamonds.

Moon diamonds are aptly named because they cannot be seen during the day. Their subtle beauty can only be observed at night. And not on any night. Only nights when there is no moon. Even the faintest light obscures their ethereal properties. You can only mine for moon diamonds for a few hours each month after the last, faintest sliver of the waning crescent moon fades and disappears completely. As soon as the new moon begins to shine, the moon diamonds disappear completely for another month. Even today with all our newfangled technology, there is still no way to find moon diamonds except by relying on your sense of touch and groping around for them with your eyes closed.

To add to Buffalo Joe's challenge, the rocky shale pit that produced the moon diamonds near his ranch was also a prime habitat for rattlesnakes. Ordinary rattlers are ornery enough for a cowpoke. These vipers were exponentially more dangerous. "How?" you ask? Well, as tumbleweeds spun and rolled across the plains, the whirling momentum built up static. The static electricity got trapped in the shale of the moon diamond mine and high tumbleweed friction ratios built up. From the highly charged landscape came shocking results. Baby snakes cracked open their insulated eggshells and slithered out, and you can positively guess the negative consequences. Some reckon it's correlation and others figure it's causation, but Buffalo Joe knew the practical outcome. Rattle snakes there were born with more than one head!

Buffalo Joe found one unusual rattler to be particularly vexing. He maintained a healthy respect for the wily serpent partly because it was a Swedish snake (having hatched near Gothenburg), and partly because it had more heads than any

other snake he had seen: seven! In honor of the snake's singular properties, Buffalo Joe named him Sven.

They say two heads are better than one, so just imagine how smart this sidewinder was with seven heads full of Swedish logic. But that was not the most troublesome issue. No siree! Humans with only an average number of heads have been scientifically verified to be 18-26%

smarter than snakes with multiple heads. The vexation was that normal rattle snakes give a fella fair warning that they're displeased by shaking their tails before they strike. Sven was enough of a sportsman to attempt to give the signal, but his seven heads tugged his tail in seven different directions and his rattle ended up paralyzed in the middle. When Sven slithered about in a pleasant mood, his rattle rattled along the sandy ground. When he became disgruntled and stopped to issue a warning, that's when he went silent. The more angry Sven became, the less noise he made.

In the still of a morning, Buffalo Joe could see Sven without needing to hear him first. In the still of a moonless night, an angry, silent Sven was nearly undetectable. To add to the challenge, a moon diamond hunt could be derailed

completely by starlight. The slightest beam made
the diamonds imperceptible. Even on the

 darkest, cloudiest nights you had to
mine with your eyes tightly closed so
as not to miss them. Buffalo Joe
blindfolded himself with his bandana to ensure
that not even the ray of a single firefly's tail
rendered his search pointless.

Buffalo Joe mined for Lilac Lilly's diamonds
by blindly sifting through the soil and rocks with

his bare hands. To
reduce the risk of an
alteration with Sven, he
set out a smorgasbord
each night. He put a cast
iron skillet of Köttbullar
meatballs ten paces from
a skillet of Flygande
Jakob. Sven would be
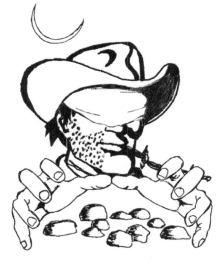
stuck in the middle all night trying to reach a
consensus between his heads on which morsel to
sample first. You might think Sven would have
always had at least a four-three majority on any
issue, but his fifth head was always changing its

mind. First Sven would slither toward the Köttbullar. Then the swing vote would change, and he's slide back toward the Flygande Jakob. Back and forth he went while Buffalo Joe mined in perfect safety.

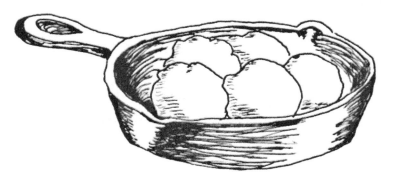

Buffalo Joe gave wide berth to the skillets and Sven as he shuffled around in the dirt on his hands and knees. Each time he felt a moon diamond, he closed his eyes even tighter lest he accidentally see it and lose sight of it. Buffalo Joe mined for months and months without opening his eyes even once. Still, he was one moon diamond short of a full necklace when he plumb ran out of new moons.

Much to his surprise, on the night before their seventeenth, eighteenth, or nineteenth anniversary, the sky put on an unexpected total lunar eclipse. Buffalo Joe rushed to find one last moon diamond. As he gathered up his mining equipment, he came to the distressing realization that he was completely out of meatballs. If he took time to prepare more, the eclipse would end before he could sift through the dust for one last moon diamond. Did he dare risk an encounter with an undetectable Sven?

Buffalo Joe hopped on Old Paint and rode as fast as that slow horse could trot. Old Paint got him to the mine with only a few minutes left before the earth's shadow released its grip on the moon. The shale pit was as quiet as a monk under a vow of silence using sign language to verbally process his thoughts. That meant Sven was very, very angry. He could smell that there was no smorgasbord that night. And even though he had never once tasted the wonderful feast because of his own indecision, tonight he laid the blame squarely on Buffalo Joe.

Buffalo Joe pleaded with the silent, invisible Sven, "If I promise to bring you Köttbullar and Flygande Jakob the day after my seventeenth, eighteenth, or nineteenth anniversary and put them next to each other so you don't have to choose, will you please let me search for moon diamonds tonight?"

Sven contemplated the offer for a moment. Then he hissed back, "Ja, sssssure, you betsssss ja."

Buffalo Joe's fingers closed around one last moon diamond just seconds before the first ray of moonlight burst from behind the umbra. He stuffed it in his shirt pocket and rode all the way home blindfolded just to be safe. Fortunately, Old Paint knew the way. Only after adding the

final diamond to Lilac Lilly's necklace, placing the jewelry in a box, hiding the box in the back corner of the closet in the

cellar, and piling blankets over the top did Buffalo Joe dare to remove the bandana from his eyes.

Lilac Lilly loved the moon diamond necklace so much that she refused to open the box lest it see the light of day. Her necklace was the most valuable piece of jewelry in the history of the world after the crown jewels of Czarina Katherine the Great, the sapphire broach of Alibaba and the forty thieves, the lapis lazuli pendants of Cleopatra, and the gilded corns of Queen Victoria's pinkie toes, in that order.

You might have never seen a moon diamond, so I'm including a drawing of Lilac Lilly's necklace on the next page. You won't be able to see the moon diamonds in the light, of course. What you need to do is wait until midnight on a cloudy, moonless night. Then close this book, wrap it in a black cloth, shove it as far under your bed as you can reach, and blindfold yourself. Then you'll be able to see the picture of Lilac Lilly's moon diamond necklace on the next page, clear as day.

And I suppose you might still think this story couldn't have happened, even after you see the necklace in the picture. I had that same thought when it was first told to me. But then I saw the underwater matches. When you see the underwater matches, you'll know for yerself.

LILAC LILLY'S
MOON DIAMOND NECKLACE

6

Buffalo Joe
and the Great Milk Shake

Buffalo Joe began his annual cattle drive late in the afternoon one morning. It was the worst part of the summer during a particularly uncomfortable heat wave. Each morning, the sun rose in a foul mood, looking for the slightest excuse to pour out its wrath on anyone wandering the Plains. By eight a.m., the sun completely lost its temper and skipped straight to the afternoon. No matter how early you got up, you still couldn't finish your morning chores before the afternoon kicked in!

Buffalo Joe enjoyed driving cattle eastward across the prairies most years. Often, he and Old Paint kept company with a herd of buffalo as they traversed the plains in the same direction. Buffalo Joe was welcomed as a native among them because of his well-known impact on the olfactory system. This particular year, he nearly missed joining with the herd.

When Buffalo Joe came within sight of the buffalo herd, he noticed they were all facing westward. As an astute observer of natural phenomena, you're thinking what Buffalo Joe thought: "They're going the wrong way." Intense sunlight has a way of playing tricks on the eyes, like creating mirages where there is no water. In fact, the sun turned the townships of Paleville and Blonde in Nebraska into Brownville and Auburn and they are called by those names to this very day!

But although the buffalo were pointed west, they were still traveling east as expected. The sun blazed so infernally bright that the herd had to walk backwards to keep the blinding light out of their eyes. They created many a new trail that year because they couldn't turn around to see where they were going and wandered in all sorts of various and sundry directions. The extreme sunlight that year is why creating new routes across the continent became known as "Trail Blazing."

The heat was full of chicanery and added urgency to Buffalo Joe's cattle drive. His longhorns needed to arrive in the more populous sectors of the state before they were barbecued on the hoof. To those who liked their steak medium rare, the cattle were mere minutes from perfection at the start of the journey. Fortunately, chuck wagon cooks preferred to serve chow that was more hearty and less tender.

Buffalo Joe reckoned that if they didn't prolong their sojourn in the parched Nebraska grasslands, they could make it to the eastern stockyards with the steers cooked only to medium-well.

When Buffalo Joe caught up to the herd of bison, he nodded a salutation. Old Paint pivoted the cattle around so their rear ends faced forward and their forward parts faced rearward. Once aligned with the bison, they commenced to moonwalk across the remainder of the territory together.

As you are well aware, I'm sure, Nebraska had ice houses all along the railroad lines in the days before electric refrigeration. Ice was cut from the surface of the lakes each winter, packed  in sawdust, and stored in places like the Armour and Company Icehouse near Memphis or the Union Pacific Icehouse in North Platte, which was the largest one ever built in the history of the world. Buffalo Joe passed through with his herd not only in the days before electricity, but before even the rail lines had been laid. There were no refrigerated icehouses yet, only ice caves.

Whenever the combined buffalo and cattle herds reached an ice cave, they stopped for a reprieve from the high temperatures. There were innumerable buffalo in the herd that summer, so it took quite a while to back them all through the opening of the cave and down deep to where the ice blocks were stacked. The radical change between searing heat and frigid cold made Buffalo Joe's cows intemperate, which made the morning chores even more difficult. In their confusion, they forgot how to be milked. Buffalo Joe had to think of a way to learn those cows all over again. After hours of breathing in the dry prairie dust churned up by the herd, Buffalo Joe hankered something fierce for a cold draught of fresh milk.

Today you can undoubtedly find all sorts of alternative milk in your general store, but it was a real challenge in the olden days. For example, there warn't no almond trees in the entire state until after Arbor Day was invented and Nebraska commenced to planting and milking trees as part of their animal husbandry. Buffalo Joe's only options were goats, oats, and stoats. He went out and lassoed some of each and walked them backwards into the ice cave.

Naturally, he milked the goats first because they were nearest in size and appearance to the cattle, and therefore the likeliest source of a refreshing beverage. Unfortunately, they got nervous and froze up and couldn't produce any better than the cows. He tried the stoats next because, as stock animals, they resembled cattle at least somewhat more than oats, which are stalk animals.

The stoats produced milk a plenty, but being of the weasel family, them critters are furry little varmints and got hair all in the milk. Many folks enjoy fizzy drinks, but no one wants fuzzy drinks! Buffalo Joe reckoned those rodents would be a bad example for the cows, so he released them back into the wild.

It's counter-intellectual fer sure, but the oats proved to be the solution. Buffalo Joe set his milking stool down next to a sheaf of freshly lassoed oats. He didn't rightly know how to go about milking oats, but luckily it was a good year for the grain harvest, and those oats were so juicy they pretty near milked themselves. When Buffalo Joe squeezed the bottom of the stalks, oat milk spurted out the top like a fountain. That's why fizzy drinks are often called "fountain drinks" to this day.

Since the oats were milking so well, Buffalo Joe decided to try the same approach with the cows. He trained his cows to lay on their backs, much to the amusement of the watching buffaloes, who could never be convinced to do something so undignified. As each cow rolled over into milking position, Buffalo Joe rewarded her with a belly scratch. Before long, Buffalo Joe was milking the cows with one hand and holding a bucket to catch the stream of cream with the other.

Every herd has at least one ornery cow, and Buffalo Joe's herd had two. Just before Buffalo Joe finished the milking, they tired of the snickers from the buffalo and kicked over one of the tin buckets in frustration. The loud clang echoed off the cave walls and spooked the buffalo. Millions of thundering hooves shook the ground violently as they stampeded backwards out of the cave. The walls vibrated and boulders crashed down from the ceiling. The supine bovine would have been in serious trouble had Buffalo Joe not been quick on his feet. He loaded up six cows on Old Paint and carried two in each arm himself as he backed out of the mouth of the cave in a hurry.

The trampling herd reversed at cataclysmic speed toward several points on the compass. In each direction they fled, the vibrations from their pounding hooves cracked the state. The worst fault line not only split Nebraska, but also spread from Kansas in the south all the way up to the Great Lakes in the northeast. Some people call it the Midcontinent Rift, but smart folks like you more accurately call it the Midcontinent Gravity Anomaly, referring to the way liquids pour up instead of down. Should you ever go spelunking with your heifers deep enough in the ice caves of that region, you'll see that milk flows upward and backward along the state's fault lines even now.

Once the buffalo settled down, the earthquake subsided, and all the longhorns were accounted for, Buffalo Joe and Old Paint retraced

their path to the epicenter in the cave where they had left the milking buckets. Much to their bemusement, the effects of the cold from the ice blocks and the shaking from the stampede had combined to turn the fresh milk into milkshakes. Buffalo Joe found it to be a much more refreshing beverage than the fuzzy drink the stoats had concocted. Milkshakes quickly became the drink of choice for all experienced trailblazers.

Although the likes of The Great Milk Shake has never been experienced since, buffalo stampedes caused several earthquakes of significance in history, including a large one the year Nebraska joined the Union. News of Buffalo Joe's heroics in saving his upside-down milk cows and the invention of frozen dairy products reached the cattle market long before he and his herd reversed down Main Street. In all the excitement, no one even noticed that, due to the delay of the stampede and the intensity of the sun that summer, Buffalo Joe's steers arrived slightly overcooked. Crowds gathered on the sidewalks to greet him, yelling, "Well done!"

It might be that you find this story about milkshakes hard to swallow. That seems fair. I felt the same way until I saw the underwater matches. When you see the matches, you'll know what's factual.

7

Buffalo Joe
and the Invisible Shadows

Buffalo Joe rode Old Paint toward town one afternoon because he needed to visit the bank. Now, you may be wondering, "Why would Old Paint need to visit a bank?" And that'd be a natural question if you didn't know he was a quarter horse. Just like he needed his mane trimmed and his hooves filed, every so often excess quarters built up and Buffalo Joe had to take him to town and deposit them in a bank account. Old Paint was slow enough anyway, but with a year's worth of quarters built up, he

 couldn't run for even a bit, or in this case, run for two bits.

Halfway into town they stopped for a rest beneath a shade tree. Buffalo Joe laid down in the cool sand to snooze for a bit, or maybe for two bits. The shady ground was pleasant enough quarters for a brief respite. When Buffalo Joe awoke, he was startled to see the back half of a horse standing a few paces away. He thought he might be dreaming. Then he thought it might be someone on the way to a costume party awaiting his partner who would be dressed as the front end of the horse.

The sand in that part of the county had a curious way of billowing in the breeze and settling down on your eyelids while you napped, so Buffalo Joe had to wipe the sleepy sand from his eyes to get a better look. He only half believed he was seeing half a quarter horse quartered in the shade, which led him to believe his sight had been reduced to a fraction and he couldn't trust it one bit. Or two bits, in this case. He walked over to consider his lack of insightfulness and was stunned to find that he was looking at the back half of Old Paint basking in the sun. Old Paint's front half disappeared completely where the shade of the tree fell across his back.

Buffalo Joe tried squinting. He tried opening his eyes wide. He tried peripheral vision and every other trick he could envision. Eventually, Old Paint's front half stepped out of the shadow into the sunlight and reappeared. Something was clearly wrong with the sun that day. Buffalo Joe was visibly shaken and could no longer see himself going to the bank that day, so he turned around and went home.

The next day, he tried again. This time, Buffalo Joe purposefully got up an hour early and took his nap immediately so he wouldn't have to break for a siesta on the ride. Something was

still wrong with the sun and the shadows were still invisible. Buffalo Joe and Old Paint passed shadow after shadow, and for some reason escaping either of their logic, whatever the shadows cast themselves on also became invisible.

Fortunately, Buffalo Joe got to the bank right at high noon when there were no shadows, or they might have never found it. He tied Old Paint at the rail outside the bank, which was right next to the town water tower. Then he unloaded the quarters and went inside to make a deposit. Just as he finished up his transaction, a masked man burst into the bank with sixguns raised. "This is a hold up!" the desperado yelled.

You're probably wondering, "How could a bank robber raise six guns all at once?" Normally, bad guys only raise one gun in each hand. Well, you're in good company because that question compounded Buffalo Joe's interest in the situation too. He could tell the teller was terrified by the sixguns and showed the telltale signs that if he lived to tell the tale, the tale would be told as far as Telluride.

Buffalo Joe himself wasn't shaken one little bit, and definitely not two little bits. He reckoned the robber would fill his bags with paper money and all of Old Paint's quarters. Those coins slowed down even a slow horse like Old Paint, so Buffalo Joe posited it would be impossible for the plunderer to outpace a posse poised to pursue him.

Sure enough, he was right. If the outlaw had stuck with dollar bills and hadn't changed his mind and taken the change, he would've got plumb away. He was no mastermind, but even he knew there was no way he was going to have a speedy getaway carrying so much weight. As all that cash was stolen money anyway, he figured he should buy more time for his escape.

Now, a normal bank robber would demand that everyone lay on the floor and close their eyes and count to a hundred before getting up and calling for the sheriff. This bandit needed twice the head start, so he ordered the teller to count to a hundred and Buffalo Joe to count

backward from a hundred. "Don't get off the floor until you meet in the middle at fifty!" he ordered them.

The crook dashed out the door and ran off down the sidewalk, tossing five of the sixguns to lessen his load. Even so, the quarters affected both the speed and trajectory of his getaway. He was carrying all the coins in his left arm and the bank notes in his right, and the uneven weight forced him to turn left at each corner.

By the time Buffalo Joe counted down to fifty, the thief was long gone. By turning left at each corner, he'd already run around the block three times! Buffalo Joe had reached fifty before the teller because he was counting backwards, which is downhill. He decided not to follow the criminal's instructions and raced out of the bank when the teller was only at thirty-two. Fortunately for Buffalo Joe, running with all that excess baggage exhausted the robber and he stopped for a spell near the water tower. While he caught his breath, Buffalo Joe ran around the block three times and caught up with him on the sunny sidewalk in front of the bank.

With only one gun, the desperado was not as formidable of an opponent as previously. Buffalo Joe had two pistols. He tried to avoid drawing weapons in a fair fight. On the other hand, hand-to-hand combat was unfavorable because the thief clearly had the advantage if it came to a wrestling match. With all those coins, he was easily three or four weight classes above Buffalo Joe.

During the bank robbery and chase, the malfunctioning sun had continued to move, as it does on most days, and the shadows had shifted. The water tower now shaded the rail where Old Paint was tied, making him completely invisible.

Buffalo Joe stood toe-to-toe with the outlaw. It's generally understood that showdowns happen at high noon, which is when Buffalo Joe arrived at the bank. It was now a quarter past the hour. Since there are 25¢ in a quarter, this particular gunfight happened at 12:25 pm instead of the traditional time. Despite the unusual hour, Old Paint had the horse sense to understand what was going on. Yes, he was a quarter horse, but he would occasionally give his two cents when he and Buffalo Joe faced a challenge. Old Paint suddenly stepped out of the invisible shadow and reappeared directly behind the robber.

"Boy howdy, am I glad to see you again!" cried Buffalo Joe.

The desperado whirled around in shock to find himself just inches from a horse who had recently had his hard-earned money stolen. He knew he was in a precarious fix between a cowboy and his horse, so he begged Old Paint, "If I drop all the money will you please let me pass?"

"Neigh!" whinnied Old Paint resolutely.

The teller emerged from the bank just then, having finally reached fifty himself. Three-to-one was insurmountable odds for the robber. He raised his hands above his head and gave up.

After escorting the criminal to the local clink, Buffalo Joe and Old Paint rode home. The bank gave them a $10 reward for apprehending the robber. After the bank fees were deducted from the reward, Buffalo Joe pocketed $2.59. Old Paint's quarters were re-deposited in the bank. No one ever figured out what went wrong with the sun that summer. Soon enough things went back to normal and invisible shadows have never been seen since.

You may not think this story can possibly be true. I'll confess, I didn't think it could've happened that way either. But then I saw the underwater matches. It's understandable for you to doubt. When you see the matches for yourself, you'll know what's true.

8

Buffalo Joe
and the Barking Cat Fish

B uffalo Joe and Old Paint were crossing the
Sand Hills early in the morning. The
weather had been unusual that spring and it
made traveling a fair bit more cumbersome. The
dew on the grass in the mornings was so thick, it
didn't evaporate before nightfall. Every morning
a new layer covered over the leftover dew from
the day before, so the old dew never had a chance
to vaporize. By the middle of spring, the

accumulated dew was as deep as Old Paint's bridle, which made slogging across the prairie a mite burdensome.

Buffalo Joe reckoned if the weather got hot, it would be at least another forty-seven days before the dew receded to the point where he could slip his boots off as he rode along and drag his toes through the cool, wet knee-high grass, as was his custom. Might take longer, but with dew that deep, it surely warn't going to take less time to dry out to a regular level of wetness.

The entire western half of Nebraska was covered in dew. You couldn't call it a flood, exactly. Floods come from rainfall, causing torrents that wash away topsoil, crops, gunny sacks, anvils, and even the occasional clothesline. This dew was a different creature all together. It was cool and refreshing to the touch and something to behold as it sparkled in the morning light. It just also happened to be hard for Old Paint to gallop through. It made life trying for Buffalo Joe and Lilac Lilly too because it was thick as molasses—somewhat less sticky, but equally difficult to do your chores in.

As Buffalo Joe rode Old Paint early that morning, he heard the far-off sound of a happy barking echoing over the Plains. A dog surely is a gleeful beast, but Buffalo Joe was surprised one could revel in delight with all the dew that kept a-comin'. The creature was almost certainly in distress of some sort, although it surely didn't sound like it.

Buffalo Joe nudged Old Paint in a starboard direction to investigate and render any assistance the animal might be inclined to accept in order to continue its jovial frivolity. Yes, it was to the starboard side they went. Buffalo Joe didn't say "hee-ya" or "whoa" that spring. He had to use nautical terminology to guide Old Paint. The dew wasn't exactly too deep for the faithful horse to walk through so much as it weighed the earth down to where Old Paint's hooves could no longer reach the ground, which had much the same effect.

When the weight of the dew was finally alleviated through a prolonged hydrological cycle, the land sprang right back and Old Paint could walk with his hooves on the ground again instead of walking twelve inches above the surface. But in the meantime, Buffalo Joe switched to nautical commands because he had removed Old Paint's saddle bags and retrofitted his faithful horse with outriggers. Since he couldn't readily find purchase for his feet, Old Paint needed a flotation device. He could swim, sure enough, but it was more efficacious to wind Old Paint's tail up tight and then let it untwist like a corkscrew propeller. Such a methodology propelled them across the state as effortlessly as steamboats navigate the Missouri River.

The USS Old Paint hadn't sailed terribly far to the starboard when he and Buffalo Joe came upon the source of the barking. It wasn't a dog at all. No sir! It was a cat with whiskers longer than your right arm (unless you're left-handed, in which case it might have come up a smidgin' short). A gray-colored cat with shiny, playful eyes—that barked! And what's more, the cat was also a fish! Scientists refer to it as a *barking cat fish*. Later, some naysayers claimed that it was only a barking catfish, which are

common in Nebraska even today, but who am I to doubt the historical reminiscences of those who saw it firsthand?

Buffalo Joe was an outdoorsman of many talents. For example, he had observed ants and learned how to burrow deep into the loamy soil, leaving behind no evidence other than a little anthill. He had also diligently considered the way corn grew in the hot summer. One afternoon, while scrutinizing the kernels under his magnifying glass, an incidental sunbeam caused a serendipitous explosion that turned the kernels into projectiles. That's how Buffalo Joe invented popcorn. Many Nebraskans claim they can hear the corn grow on especially hot summer nights. Buffalo Joe not only listened, he spoke back! Using the corn's own native speech, he taught the stalks on his farm to reach for the sun. Each autumn, the ears that grew under his tutelage were allowed to move their tassels and matriculate to the grain bin.

By the time he came across the barking cat fish, Buffalo Joe could speak many Mid-Western tongues. He communicated quite freely not only with corn, but also with several species of tubers, a handful of squashes, half a dozen orchard trees,

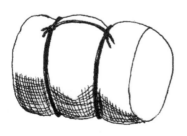 and liverwurst. Some say "Baloney!" but it was actually liverwurst, which is far more difficult for native English speakers to master.

Buffalo Joe also spoke the languages of Antish, Old Paintian, Pollywoguese, Wolfan, and various and sundry invertebrate languages such as Crawdadish. It was precisely because he spoke Wolfan fluently that Buffalo Joe thought he would be able to speak with the barking cat fish. And communicate they did.

Many a day that spring began with the sunrise and Buffalo Joe's greeting to his new friend rocketing across the dew-soaked plains. In fact, all days in all seasons start with sunrise in Nebraska. But not all start out with a hearty, "Icky-icky-kai-yai-yaaaaaaaaaaaaaay!" And even fewer continue after such a start with a barking cat fish returning the salutation with a whooping "Akky-icky-akky-ikky-ish-mish-humphhh!"

The dew eventually began to recede in the Territory to such a degree that the corkscrew tail method of propulsion was becoming ever less productive for Old Paint. The outriggers were only useful for Buffalo Joe and Lilac Lilly to carry him through the treacherous turpentine pits to the south of their homestead. Many a dinosaur, not a few woolly mammoths, and precisely one

dozen three-toed sloths became fossilized in
Nebraska by unwarily stepping into tar pits in
prehistoric times.

In historic times, the tar thinned and diluted
into turpentine. You know how turpentine
interacts with old paint! Buffalo Joe didn't want
his faithful horse to dissolve into nothing, so he
would grab one end of the outriggers while Lilac
Lilly lifted the other. Together, they'd carry Old
Paint across the turpentine pits in safety.

The barking cat fish lived in a pond on the
other side of the turpentine pits, and it was too
far to carry Old Paint on a regular basis. So,
Buffalo Joe regretfully had to settle for daily
conversational yelling across the frontier. Soon
the grass became too tall to even call across the
wilderness. If it was normal grass, it might not
have made a difference, but this was saw grass.
The blades were sharp enough to cut the call
every time Buffalo Joe tried to converse with his
new friend. His "Icky-icky-kai-yai-yaaaaaaay"
might make it one mile or even five miles, but no
matter how high he shouted, eventually a blade
of grass sliced his words into confetti, and they

drifted silently down onto the surface of the turpentine and were never heard again.

To this day, no one ever hears the reply "Akky-ikky-akky-ikky-ish-mish-humphhh" from the barking cat fish across the turpentine pits. If you don't believe me, go outside with a group of friends as witnesses and yell Buffalo Joe's call at the top of your lungs in the direction of the Nebraska panhandle. I sincerely promise you'll not hear the reciprocal answer waft back on the wind.

The saw grass grew so treacherous and caused so much consternation that when the telegraph came through the state, they had to bring in swashbucklers who sword-fought with each and every blade of grass until the grasses were cut down and incarcerated. Unfortunately, due to governmental incompetency and bureaucratic mismanagement, the resulting hay was let out on bale.

Buffalo Joe decided he enjoyed his morning discourse with the barking cat fish too much to surrender to antagonistic plants without trying a trick or two himself. He invited his grandchildren round to the ranch to figure out a solution to the vexing conundrum. Necessity is the mother of invention, as they say.

Who Buffalo Joe and Lilac Lilly's children might have been remains a mystery lost in antiquity. General consensus and scholarly opinion are in full agreement that Buffalo Joe and Lilac Lilly were wise and knowing folk, and so they may not have had children at all. They understood that being a grandpa and grandma is the best job in the world, so they may have skipped right to dessert, so to speak, and had their grandchildren first.

Jedediah, Jehoshaphat, Methuselah, Melchizedek, Abishag, Hulda, Kezia and A-Bun-in-the-Oven all came when summoned, as did a score of Buffalo Joe's other grandchildren. It was quickly decided that Buffalo Joe would tie a nylon fishing line through the buttonholes where his youngest granddaughter's suspenders attached to her britches. With a mighty cast the likes of which has never been seen west of the sunrise, Buffalo Joe launched her from the tip of his fishing pole up and over the turpentine-drenched saw grass toward the pond where his partner in the subtle arts of banter resided.

Now, even Buffalo Joe could only cast ten miles on a good day. When his granddaughter started arching back down toward the earth, she flapped her arms for a little extra lift. You're probably thinking, "Humans can't fly." And you are correct. But she didn't need to fly—only stretch her downward trajectory a little farther in a horizontal fashion, gaining a few extra miles. The little girl splashed down in the deepest part of the pond, where barking cat fish are wont to while away the hours as a steady stream of krill, plankton, and tinned peaches drift with the current into their mouths, slide past their gullets, and lodge satisfyingly in their tummies.

Although it is widely reported that Buffalo Joe's granddaughter was as lovely as my own granddaughters, she unfortunately did not speak Wolfan. It was of no consequence that she had reached a proficiency level in Cornish. They were from two different language families, one zoological and the other botanical. To solve that problem, Buffalo Joe had fashioned a dog whistle for her to use. They say that only dogs can hear dog whistles but that is a distortion of the truth. A barking cat fish comprehends them with just as much ease.

Buffalo Joe's granddaughter sank down, down, down, down, down into the barking cat fish's pond. She descended so far that, unbeknownst to her, Buffalo Joe's grandsons were unlacing their shoes and handing the shoestrings to their grandpa to extend the line. The boys fetched kitchen towels, sheets, and any other garments that were somewhat elongated to add to the line. The girls lined up shoulder-to-shoulder and braided their pigtails together in a chain to make the last few yards of line their little cousin needed to reach the very bottom of the barking cat fish's pond.

As the little girl floated weightlessly next to a can of tinned peaches, she put the dog whistle to her lips and transmitted Buffalo Joe's morning greeting. The barking cat fish was so overjoyed to have this new channel of communication that his reply echoed off the Rockies and bounced back as far as Paducah, Kentucky, "AKKY-IKKY-AKKY-IKKY-ISH-MISH-HUMPHHH!" Some modern ranchers say that if you lay your ear in the waves that lap a certain creek bank in the Panhandle, you can still hear the jubilation rippling in the foam.

You might like to try to spin a yarn with that barking cat fish someday. He is a clever conversationalist if you speak Wolfan, or perhaps a dialect of Tuberese. They say he has become bilingual over the past century. If you don't speak anything other than English, that's okay. Get yourself a dog whistle and put the tip in the water of the pond just south of the turpentine pits. But you know how when you whistle with your lips, the pitch changes depending on whether you blow out or suck in? Well, a dog whistle doesn't have the right pitch for a barking cat fish if you

blow through it. You have to suck the air in. So
put that whistle in just below the surface of the

deepest part of
the pond and
suck in just like
you were sipping
through a straw.
If you're lucky,

before long you just might hear his reply.

If you're like me, you're skeptical about the
veracity of this historical recollection. I can tell
you that I did not believe it until I saw the
underwater matches. And I don't blame you if
you doubt it's true until you see the underwater
matches for yourself.

9

Buffalo Joe
and the Snoring Dirt

Buffalo Joe was occasionally called upon to give lectures at the local primary school, county fair, state legislature, portioning of the Austro-Hungarian Empire, or after-church potluck dinner, which happened on the third Sunday after the first full moon of spring. He was a humble man who didn't flash his extensive learnin', but he believed his understanding of the soils of Box Butte County and their rascally personalities could be of some benefit to those hankering for a better tomorrow.

The school marm would frequently call him in to teach the young'uns, who often got distracted playing in the schoolyard. As they jumped rope they would, more often than not, kick up a fair-sized cloud of dust. And although neither the dust nor the jump rope had anything to do with the school marm, the children incorporated her name in their endless rope-skipping rhymes:

Miss Missy has no mister,
But she has a silly sister.

Miss Missy's former mister's
Ranch got swept up by a twister.

Miss Missy missed that mister,
So she chased the messy twister.

Miss Missy's silly sister
Missed her and Miss Missy's mister.

The children would become so engrossed in their game and the image of a wobbly tornado careening across the prairie with a ranch balanced on its tip-top like a Sunday hat that Miss Missy could hardly get their attention to call them back to class. If her efforts failed, she would invite Buffalo Joe to lecture the children on the wonders of airborne dust and the refractionary properties of light dispersion amidst flotational particles—which, as you know, is of keen interest to first, second, and third graders. Buffalo Joe was always happy to provide the children with a scientific education, and they were always happy to attend to his lessons with rapt attention.

The minister of Box Butte Community Church called on Buffalo Joe at the potlucks because it was his habit to preach on the Parable of the Sower and the Seed each planting season. Buffalo Joe could make simple the deep truths of various topsoils, loams, peats, substrates, and everyday garden-variety dirt. He was an astute observer of biblical passages on some occasions and believed that man was made from the dust of the ground. He had also heard that you are what you eat. Like a flash of lightning, he put two and two together and invented mud pies to help mankind replenish the nutrients their earthly bodies craved. Many historians believe Buffalo Joe's simple exhortations were more'n likely the cause of the great spiritual revivals that swept the Panhandle as swiftly and thoroughly as Miss Missy's messy twister.

As to why the Austro-Hungarian Empire enlisted his self-taught erudition—well, that has been a much-discussed topic in institutions of high learnin' throughout much of the Americas, Central Europe, southern Antarctica, and more than a few outlying suburbs of New Delhi. Buffalo Joe, in later years, would simply explain, "They needed a new boundary that would stay in place. I chose the spot where the mud was the least slippery and so the boundary was least likely to slide downhill when gravity tugged at it." In both Austro-Hungary and in the Nebraska Unicameral, Buffalo Joe had a way of cleaning up dirty politics.

Buffalo Joe's audiences were sometimes perplexed by all manner of nuances in the esoteric understanding of dirt. For example, when Buffalo Joe would begin explaining the principles of snoring dirt to regular folks, they would say such nonsensical things as, "Do you mean boring dirt?" Boring dirt is far less interesting than snoring dirt, as you might have presumed by the name. Buffalo Joe did know a thing or two about boring dirt because he had observed it conscientiously for more than seventy years. At times, the boring dirt reached the verge of becoming interesting, but it always disappointed in the end. As boring dirt eroded over the years, it might come close to shaping itself into Mandarin characters or Viking runes, but at the last minute it only spelled out plain old English. Even worse, it only spelled out sayings that were already as common as dirt. No sir, snoring dirt was not to be confused with boring dirt.

Predictably, the next fella in the crowd would yell, "Do you mean flooring dirt?" Buffalo Joe had patience even with such banal hecklers because he knew all people, though they be made of dirt and in need of the occasional mud pie, were created in the image of their Creator. "No," Buffalo Joe would explain, "flooring dirt is the dirt we all have in our sod houses." It's true that flooring dirt was also in everyone's bedrooms, but that didn't mean it snored. After all, in the days of one-room sod houses, everyone's bedroom was also their kitchen, lounge room, dining room, hallway, billiard room, library, study, ballroom, conservatory, and man cave.

By and by, a bystander would finally shush the crowd so Buffalo Joe could give them the dirt on Box Butte County dirt. As the crowd stilled to listen, they invariably marveled how anyone could take on such a layered topic as soils and make it clear as mud.

Snoring dirt, as the townsfolk soon came to know, could only be found snoozing in western Nebraska. Few homesteaders ever dreamed they would encounter it. Buffalo Joe was an expert on snoring dirt because he suffered from the affliction of sleepwalking. Snoring dirt obviously didn't snore in waking hours. To this day, sleepwalking remains the only sure way to consciously observe a robust specimen in action.

Night after night, Buffalo Joe wandered the lonely prairies of western Nebraska with nothing on his feet except his cowboy boots. At first, he didn't believe Lilac Lilly when she told him that he traversed the ranges with the tumbleweeds every night. But each morning, he noticed his dirty boots beside his bed and his squeaky-clean feet. The dusty state of the boots was a compelling witness that they had been out perambulating during the night, and Buffalo 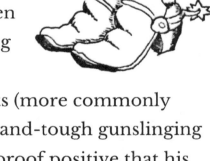 Joe's unsoiled pedal digits (more commonly referred to in the rough-and-tough gunslinging West as "tootsies") were proof positive that his feet had been inside those boots as they did so.

One night, Buffalo Joe walked miles and miles, almost to the border of the Wyoming Territory. It was during that stroll that he saw the formation of a wonderful megalith. The soil was snoring so loudly, it sounded like boulders crashing, bashing, and grinding. It was fortunate that Buffalo Joe was a heavy sleeper, or the racket would most certainly have woken him, and he wouldn't have been asleep enough to see that marvelous masterpiece form. The soil blew out dust, gravel, rocks, stones, and intermittent hairballs with each seismic snore. Up and up, higher and higher, the heap heaved heavenward.

By the time the sun came up, the stone pillar reached the sky. Subsequent settlers, passing by in wagon trains on the Oregon Trail, gave the monument the misnomer "Chimney Rock." They weren't observant enough in their sleep to ascertain the real cause of the formation, and so gave it that unsuitable moniker. They further proved their shortage of intelligentsia by leaving

Nebraska. They were so gullible as to believe they could find a better place to live.

Over the years, Buffalo Joe found many uses for snoring dirt. The second most famous was as a test for sleepwalking. You may not think this to be an accurate assessment, but try out his theory before jumping to a conclusion. Place a pair of cowboy boots beside your bed each night for a week. If you wake up in the morning and find that your shoes have even a sprinkling of dust, but your feet are squeaky clean, then you're a confirmed sleepwalker. That's the only way you can know for sure. Someone might tell you that you walked in your sleep, but it could always just be a tall tale without the clean feet to prove it.

Buffalo Joe discovered perhaps the most famous use for snoring dirt one night when he walked so far, he fell asleep in his sleep. When he half woke up from the second sleep, he realized he needed a snack to give him energy to walk home. On arriving, he'd have to wake up another one and a half times and start the morning chores before breakfast. He gathered some snoring dirt in a tin and made a mud pie by pouring water from his canteen into the mixture. That pie has got to have been the most nutritious mud pie

ever made because it gave Buffalo Joe the energy to walk from the southern end of the state near northern Kansas to the northern end of the state near southern South Dakota and back home without stirring in his sleep.

The mud pie was so nourishing that he only ate half. The other half was still in his mouth the next morning. It prevented Buffalo Joe from uttering any nocturnal cacophony, referred to by most folk as "snoring." Lilac Lilly awoke as refreshed and invigorated as Buffalo Joe that morning due to the lack of snoring. She slept well enough when he was out on his midnight wanderings, but in the wee morning hours it was harder to slumber restfully.

Now, Buffalo Joe was no medical doctor. No, he was a simple connoisseur of soils. Yet many a folk followed his recommendation to cure their own night-time ailments. You might try it too. Simply eat half a mud pie before bedtime and leave the remaining half in your mouth. Should you wake up with your mouth still full of mud, you may rest assured that you didn't snore and upset the missus.

So it was that Buffalo Joe became an itinerate lecturer on soils. You might think this story isn't true and I wouldn't blame you. I didn't believe it myself until I saw the underwater matches. Don't you believe it either until you see them underwater matches for yourself!

10

Buffalo Joe
and the Year-Long Christmas

Buffalo Joe was counting down the days until winter. He was counting down the days until Christmas too, because Christmas morning comes only a few days after winter's arrival. The days were ticking by fast because, as you know, the days get shorter as winter sets in. The sun was up for only nine hours each day, which meant each day passed in five less hours than in the summer when the days were fourteen hours long.

The shorter days were fine with Buffalo Joe because it meant that Christmas was going to come all that much sooner. He was excited to celebrate with Lilac Lilly. Buffalo Joe had made her a new coffee pot and could barely wait for her to pull the brightly wrapped box from under the tree and open it. He had spent the better part of the autumn making the coffee pot.

In the days of yesteryear, no general stores had been opened yet in western Nebraska. Sears and Roebuck catalogues were still decades in the future. As sure as bucking bales into the hayloft was a long and arduous chore, giving the perfect Christmas gift was no easy undertaking. You couldn't simply mail off an order form and four shiny pennies with the Pony Express rider and expect your coffee pot to arrive in six to eight weeks on the Wells Fargo wagon. No sir! Back when Nebraska was still a territory, creativity and ingenuity were required for making gifts.

The idea of the coffee pot as a gift for Lilac Lilly had come to Buffalo Joe back in late August during a thunderstorm. The sky was so dark and ominous that day, you couldn't hardly see beyond the brim of your ten-gallon hat. Buffalo Joe had lined up miles of fence that afternoon by tapping each post a few inches into the soil with his 175-pound sledgehammer. He had developed a powerful thirst by the time the clouds let loose, so he pulled his tin cup out of his saddlebags and set it on a fence post to catch a raindrop.

The rain came down so heavy and fast that when a drop hit the top of a fence post, it drove it two feet deeper into the ground. The drops were so big that Buffalo Joe only needed one to fill that tin cup. Sure as shootin', a raindrop the size of a mule skinner's hind end came down in a triangular fashion and landed squarely in the round cup.

Well, don't you know, just as hastily as it plopped into the cup, it was snatched back out by the driving wind. Buffalo Joe watched that drop fly back up into the sky, loop around fifty feet in the air, and roil around with the leaves, woodchips, silage, and other debris being driven

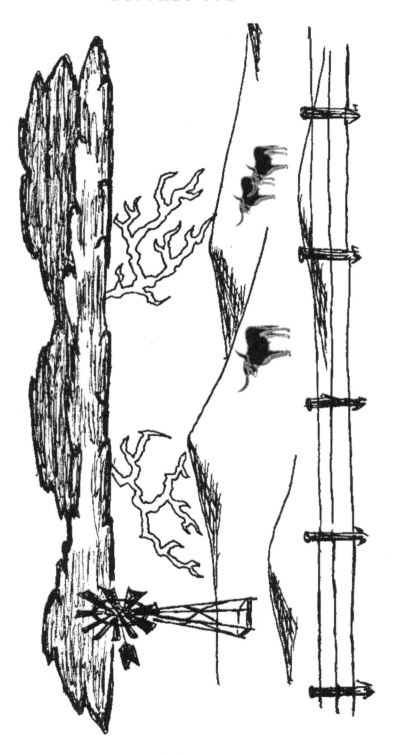

like Longhorn steers across the Panhandle. That wily raindrop spun through the late summer storm like butter in a churn.

Buffalo Joe realized that the viscous saps and flavors of that aerial slurry were seeping into the raindrop, and it was percolating into a robust brew stronger than any cowboy coffee that has ever been roasted over a cattleman's campfire.

Buffalo Joe was parched to the point of desiccated fossilization in the middle of that downpour, and he wasn't about to let that drop of water escape over the horizon. He jumped on Old Paint, who especially smelled like old paint, being drenched by the howling squall. "HEE-YA!" yelled Buffalo Joe and Old Paint shot off like lightening. More like spent lightning faded out to no more than a blind spot in the center of your vision. He was an old horse, and although he was faithful, he was not fast.

Old Paint plodded across the prairie and soon caught up to that whirling, brewing drop of water. Buffalo Joe reached his tin cup out and caught the raindrop before it hit the ground, seeped into the Ogallala Aquifer, and was lost for good until the invention of center pivot irrigation.

As he put the mug up to his lips, Buffalo Joe reined Old Paint around and headed into the wind to retrace his trail toward home. But before

he could take a gulp, the wind gusted with menacing tenacity. Buffalo Joe leaned forward to stay atop his horse. The blast hit so hard that it scoured the week-old razor stubble from his left cheek, leaving him clean shaven on the windward side and scruffy on the other. It also ripped the raindrop out of the cup and heaved it back into the tempest.

Buffalo Joe was mighty thirsty by then. "HEE-YA!" he cried again. Off plodded Old Paint, pursuing the raindrop as if it were prey. Out went the tin cup once again to capture that ornery raindrop. This time it was darker and sludgier than before. Up came the wind. Out flew the brew. "HEE-YA!" Plod—plop—whoosh, plod—

plop—whoosh, the game of catch and release continued all afternoon.

Old Paint galloped faster than the wind as day wore into evening. Faster than the wind after it had died down completely, at any rate. Down came that rascally raindrop they had chased across several neighboring counties. Out reached the tin cup for the ten dozenth time. And splat went the drop into the tin cup for the final time.

It was the best cup of coffee Buffalo Joe had ever tasted. It was so thick he had to take out his pocketknife and slice off chunks to drink. He swallowed the last lump just as he reached the new fence line he was laying when the storm came up. Much to his dismay, the fierce winds had blown down his fence. The barbed wire  was jumbled into a ruined tangle beyond his ability to remedy, although he did give it a mighty good try.

Buffalo Joe sucked in as much air as he could hold. Then he sucked in more—and then more and more until he ballooned up so big and round that his belly button turned inside out. He held his breath until he thought he would burst. Then—with index fingers wedged in his ears and the tips of his thumbs up his nose to prevent even a tiny bit of air pressure from escaping— he blew like a discharge of TNT on the mangled fence from the opposite direction as the gale. It almost worked, too. The fence posts blew back into their holes. The barbed wire unraveled, and the nails flew back and tacked it to the posts. But it was all for naught. No metal can go through that much stress without losing what those hifalutin, starched-collared varmints at the assayer's office called "tinsel strength." The fence warn't no longer durable enough to hold in the livestock.

In frustration, Buffalo Joe picked up a length of barbed wire and began chewing it. The wind had worn the grass from the pasture just as cleanly as his windward cheek, so there was nothing else to chew on as he pondered what to do. He was lost so deeply in his pensive considerations, he chewed the wire down to a

nub. As he cyphered how in tarnation a Great
Plains thunderhead could brew up such a
satisfying cup of coffee while simultaneously
compromising his valuable fencing materials, an
idea formed. The idea rattled around in his
cowboy hat for a spell, but eventually it found its
way in between his ears and roosted there like a
hen at dusk.

Soon Buffalo Joe had thunk it all out. If he
was careful with the sharp barbs, he could chew
all the wire flat between now and Christmas Day.
He could then weave the masticated metal into

the shape of a coffee pot as a gift for Lilac Lilly. She had been yearning for a perfect cup of coffee since childhood, as her mother and father retold the story of them each leaving their home countries and travelling around the world, one headed north and the other south, until they met in Nebraska with nothing left in their knapsacks except eight and twelve ounces of roasted coffee beans, respectively.

No coffee pot in the Territory seemed capable of brewing a cup with just the right combination of flavor, viscosity, and roughage. Buffalo Joe had a hunch a coffee pot made of storm-seasoned barbed wire would do just the trick. So, he got to chewin', and he chewed for many long months because he didn't want his efforts to amount to gnaw-thing.

Winter arrived a few days before Christmas that year, as it does in most cases, except leap years that are divisible by three. It was the coldest winter ever anywhere in the known world south of the North Pole. Christmas Eve morning dawned colder and more frigid still. Buffalo Joe tried to light a fire with one of his underwater matches, but the flame froze solid on the tip of the matchstick. He tried rubbing the flame in his palms to warm it up, but to no avail. There was nothing for it but to put the match in his pocket to try to thaw the flame out enough to light the kindling in the potbellied stove. He needed fire. For warmth, yes, but also so Lilac Lilly could try her new coffee pot on the morrow when they opened their presents. Buffalo Joe wasn't in the mood to invent iced coffee.

By noon on Christmas Eve, even the snow was asking to come indoors to warm up. Buffalo Joe saddled up Old Paint and rode off in search of water for the coffee pot. I'm assuming you're putting two and two together and hypothesizing there wouldn't be any liquid water around on a day that could freeze fire. And you aren't remiss in your thinking. Nor was Buffalo Joe. The snow drifts on the Plains were shivering and blowing every-which-way and could not be wrangled into the coffee pot, so he went in search of a more reliable water source.

Buffalo Joe was still warming the lit match in his pocket when he reached Rat and Beaver Lake.

After attaching a chain to a hooked spike he had hammered into the ice, he gave Old Paint the spurs. Old Paint lurched forward so hard he pulled the whole frozen lake out in one big block of ice. They dragged it back to the ranch scraping a huge ditch all the way. It was hard work for an old horse, and he staggered from time to time, but he kept at it.

After Christmas, Buffalo Joe repeated the process at Mud Lake, Lake McConaughy, Pawnee Lake, Plum Creek, Jeffrey Reservoir, and many more. Each time, Buffalo Joe used his spurs. Each time, Old Paint pulled an entire frozen lake out of its bed and dragged it home, leaving meandering channels from one end of Nebraska to the other that later became the Platte River.

When Buffalo Joe arrived home from that very first trip to Rat and Beaver Lake, it was coming up on the stroke of midnight. Christmas was almost here. After putting Old Paint away in the barn, Buffalo Joe broke off a chunk of lake ice and slipped quietly into the sod house so as not to wake Lilac Lilly. He didn't take his muddy boots off at the door. Quite the contrary. Tracking mud into a sod house lays down a fresh coat of mud on the floor, keeping it shiny and bright. Buffalo Joe took the lit match out of his pocket, and it was just barely warm enough to start a fire in the potbellied stove. Then he put the hunk of ice in a pot to liquify. The final thing Buffalo Joe did before snuggling into bed next to Lilac Lilly that night was to flip the daily calendar over to December 25th.

Well, wouldn't you know! That match lit the potbellied stove all right, but the bitter winter brawled like a sidewinder all night long trying to put out the flame. By morning, they had come to an uneasy stalemate. Winter froze everything in that little house except the fire in the stove, the pot of lake water, the Christmas tree, and the brightly wrapped coffee pot underneath. Everything else was frozen solid except for Buffalo Joe and Lilac Lilly themselves, who were toasty warm under their buffalo skin blankets.

Yep, you're figuring right. The calendar was frozen in place, as was time itself. If Buffalo Joe hadn't fortuitously turned the calendar before he nodded off the night before, time would have solidified on the 24th and Christmas would not have come at all that year. As it was, the little stove kept them warm every day for a whole year. And every day for a whole year, it was Christmas Day.

Buffalo Joe and Lilac Lilly unwrapped gifts the first morning of the year-long Christmas. Lilac Lilly loved the coffee pot because it was a one-of-a-kind gift contrived especially for her. No other cookhouse utensil was, or ever would be, just like it. It had teeth marks in it that could be linked forensically to her husband. Well, him and Old Paint, who helped too. It was a lot of barbed wire, after all.

I'm guessing that you probably don't believe this story. I didn't either when I first heard it. But then I saw the underwater matches. I would expect you to reserve your judgment, too, until you see the underwater matches for yourself.

ABOUT THE AUTHOR

Grandpa Dan wasn't always this old. He grew up on the edge of town, roaming the countryside until dark. He was educated formally in history and theology. Informally, he learned to ride a horse along the banks of the Platte River, pull a calf in Cass County, hunt whitetail deer in Calamus West, and lay underground power lines with Burt Co. Public Power District. Blessed by "the good life," he now invests his time encouraging others.